In Rosa's Mexico

by Campbell Geeslin

illustrated by Andrea Arroyo

Alfred A. Knopf
New York

For all the girls: Lyn, Meg, Liz, Lucy, and Eliza
—C.G.

To Maru Esquivel, mi madre, with love
—A.A.

THIS IS A BORZOI BOOK PUBLISHED BY ALFRED A. KNOPF, INC.

Text copyright © 1996 by Campbell Geeslin
Illustrations copyright © 1996 by Andrea Arroyo
All rights reserved under International and Pan-American Copyright Conventions. Published in
the United States of America by Alfred A. Knopf, Inc., New York, and simultaneously in Canada
by Random House of Canada Limited, Toronto. Distributed by Random House, Inc., New York.

Library of Congress Cataloging-in-Publication Data

Geeslin, Campbell.
In Rosa's Mexico / by Campbell Geeslin ; illustrated by Andrea Arroyo.
p. cm.
Summary: Three stories about a Mexican girl's encounters with a rooster, a burro, and a wolf.
Each story uses some Spanish words, which are listed in the brief "Spanish-English dictionary."
ISBN 0-679-86721-X (trade) — ISBN 0-679-96721-4 (lib. bdg.)
[1. Mexico—Fiction. 2. Animals—Fiction.] I. Arroyo, Andrea, ill. II. Title.
PZ7.G25845In 1996
[Fic]-dc20 94-45092

Printed in Singapore
10 9 8 7 6 5 4 3 2 1

http://www.randomhouse.com/

Spanish-English Glossary

anillo *(a-NEE-yoh)*: ring

burro *(BOOR-oh)*: donkey

estrella *(ess TRAY-ya)*: star

fiesta *(fee ESS-ta)*: party

el gallo *(el GUY-yoh)*: the rooster

el lobo *(el LOH-boh)*: the wolf

olla *(AW-ya)*: cooking pot

río *(REE-yoh)*: river

sí *(see)*: yes

sopa *(SOH-pa)*: soup

tía *(TEE-ya)*: aunt

violetas *(vee-oh-LET-tas)*: violets

Rosa and El Gallo

El Gallo crows. Rosa wakes.
She picks violetas on the mountain.
She walks to town and sells them.
Rosa buys meat for the sopa in the olla.

One night the mountain rumbles.

In the morning El Gallo crows.
Rosa wakes. She goes to pick violetas,
but ashes cover all.

Rosa's mama asks,
"Where is the meat for the sopa?"
Rosa says, "Ashes fell last night.
I had no violetas to sell."
Mama says, "We must eat.
Go get El Gallo for the olla."

Rosa says to El Gallo, "Good-bye, my morning music."
El Gallo opens his beak, and out fly violetas.
Rosa gathers them as they fall,
sells them in town, and buys meat.

Now, every morning,
El Gallo crows violetas.
And there is always meat
for the sopa in the olla.

One morning the olla cracks, and out spills the sopa.
The fire hisses and dies.
"I will make a new olla," Rosa tells her mama.

Outside, there is a crash.
Pedro's old burro, loaded with wood,
falls in the road and cannot get up.
Rosa goes to the río for clay.

She rolls it into a long, long rope

and coils it around and around into an olla.

At Tía's house, Rosa heaps sticks around the olla.

Tía sets the sticks ablaze and bakes the olla.

Rosa takes her new olla home.
The poor burro still lies where he fell.

That night, while Rosa sleeps,
her new olla uncoils.
Rosa grabs hold as the clay rope climbs out the window.

Up, up, up into the heavens she goes.
She picks a small estrella and puts it in her pocket.

The next morning Rosa presses the estrella
onto the burro's forehead.
He jumps up and trots off into town!
At the río Rosa fills the new olla.
It does not leak.

Rosa goes to the río for water.
El Lobo is caught in a trap.
She sets him free. He thanks her
and promises to repay her.
The next morning,
there is a golden anillo
on her windowsill,
and Rosa puts it on her finger.

On the way into town with her violetas,
Rosa meets a beautiful bride who is weeping.
"I have lost my wedding anillo!" the bride cries.

Rosa asks, "Is this it?"
"Oh, sí!" says the happy bride.
"Now come to my wedding fiesta."
Rosa says, "I must sell my violetas."
The bride says, "My husband will buy all of them."

So Rosa goes to the fiesta.
There are six guitars and a white cake.
Everyone dances.

The next morning, El Lobo appears at Rosa's window.
"Why aren't you wearing the anillo I gave you?" El Lobo asks.
Rosa says, "It belonged to a bride, and I gave it back."

El Lobo howls, "Ohoooo! Bad! Bad! Bad!"
He did not want Rosa to know that he is a thief.
And so to make her forget the stolen anillo,
he gives her his own silk pillow.

Now, every night, Rosa sleeps on El Lobo's pillow
and dreams of golden anillos with wings.